MY BROTHER'S KEEPER

TOM AND TONY
BRADMAN

A & C BLACK
AN IMPRINT OF BLOOMSBURY
LONDON NEW DELHI NEW YORK SYDNEY

MY BROTHER'S KEEPER

This edition published 2014 by

A & C Black, an imprint of Bloomsbury Publishing Plc

50 Bedford Square, London, WC1B 3DP

www.bloomsbury.com

Bloomsbury is a registered trademark of Bloomsbury Publishing Plc

ISBN 978-1-4081-9679-3

A CIP catalogue for this book is available from the British Library.

Printed and bound by CPI Group (UK) Ltd, Croydon CR0 4YY

3 5 7 9 10 8 6 4

MIX
Paper from
responsible sources
FSC
www.fsc.org   FSC® C020471

CONTENTS

Chapter One

A Great Adventure

Alfie Barnes peered into the darkness shrouding no-man's land and wished he were taller. Like the rest of the men in his section he was in position on the trench's fire-step, but he could only just get his head up to the level of the sandbagged parapet. As for using his rifle if they were attacked – well, that would be almost impossible.

He could hear the usual rumbling of the big guns in the distance. Ours, not theirs, he thought, having learned the difference over the last few weeks. There was a burst of machine-gun fire somewhere, a sound that made him think of thick cardboard being ripped. That wasn't close either, but Alfie still gripped his rifle more tightly.

'Hey, Ernie!' he said to the man on his left. 'Can you see anything?'

Ernie turned to look at him. Only a silvery sliver of moon and a few faint stars shone in the night sky, so Ernie's face was in shadow beneath his canvas-covered helmet. Their breath formed small clouds of white mist in the cold air.

'Pipe down, Alfie!' Ernie hissed. 'Do you want to get us killed?'

'Keep your hair on, Ernie,' muttered Cyril, the next man along. 'Old Fritz ain't interested, mate. He's still tucked up nice and warm in his dugout.'

'Oh yeah?' said George, the man beyond Cyril. 'You never know with Fritz. A whole division of Prussian Guards might be creeping up on us right now.'

Alfie turned back to examine no-man's land, excitement suddenly coursing through him. Maybe this was it, the moment when he would actually do some fighting – after all, that was what he'd joined up for, wasn't it? Half an hour before dawn every day the two hundred and fifty men of the company had a 'stand-to' along the three hundred yards of trench they occupied, then again at dusk, the most likely times for an assault. But there had been no attacks since Alfie had arrived in the line, and his excitement seeped away as he realised nothing was going to happen this morning, either. The sky was slowly growing lighter in the east, a pale sun casting its feeble glow on the shell craters and tangles of rusting barbed wire that separated the British and German trenches. There were no living men in no-man's land, only the scattered, rotting corpses of the dead.

'You're an evil swine, George,' said Cyril. 'Always teasing the lad.'

'You don't care, do you, Alfie?' said George. 'You like it, really.'

George looked round Cyril and Ernie to wink at Alfie, and the boy grinned. It was true, he didn't mind. Most men felt it was their duty to tease young lads – such was the natural order of things. Alfie had suffered worse back in England, or Blighty as his new mates had taught him to call it. His dad was a porter in Covent Garden market and had got him a job there when Alfie had left school at the age of twelve. The other porters had teased him relentlessly, but it had all been in fun.

There was more light now, the sky turning a bruised grey, and word came along the line to stand down. Alfie slung his rifle over his back and jumped off the fire-step, avoiding the deep puddle of mud filling the trench bottom at that point. He followed his mates to the dugout they shared, a shallow cave scooped in the side of the trench and half screened off with an old bit of sacking. Inside were four empty ammunition boxes they used as seats and some planks they took it in turns to sleep on.

'Do your stuff, Alfie,' said George, lighting a fag. 'I'm dying for a brew.'

Ernie lit one of his roll-ups and Cyril puffed at his pipe. They'd all been on at Alfie to smoke since he'd arrived, and he'd tried it once, but didn't like the way it had made him cough and feel dizzy. He filled the kettle with water from a five-gallon petrol can and set it on the blue flame of their small primus cooker, a treasure they guarded fiercely. Cookers were few and far between, and most of the other men used candles stuck in dixie tins to boil their kettles, which took a long time. Alfie and his mates, however, could have their hands round warm mugs of tea in a few minutes.

He looked at them now in the pale morning light, these three young men who had taken care of him since he'd arrived at the Front. George was dark and wiry and full of jokes; Cyril was big and fair and liked his creature comforts; and Ernie was skinny and ginger and a worrier. All three were wrapped up against the cold, with sheepskins or leather jerkins over their uniform tunics, scarves round their necks and extra pairs of socks under their puttees and boots. Alfie was kitted out similarly, thanks to them. They had scrounged whatever he needed, and taught him an awful lot too.

But then he was only fifteen, and daft to be there, as George was always telling him. Alfie didn't agree. It had been the best day of his life when he'd joined the crowd at the recruitment drive in Lewisham Town Hall and persuaded the sergeant to sign him up. 'How old are you, son?' the big red-faced man had said. 'Nineteen, sir!' Alfie had replied, knowing that was the age you had to be. Alfie was short and scrawny and knew he looked young, even for a fifteen-year-old, so it had been a tricky moment. 'I suppose I'll have to take your word for it,' the sergeant had said, grinning.

Alfie's mum had been very upset, but his dad had shaken him by the hand and said he was proud to have such a brave son. The family had seen him off at the station when he'd left for training camp, his mum and younger brothers and sisters sobbing their eyes out. He hadn't cried, though. He was going to fight for his country, to make sure the Huns wouldn't come marching up Lewisham High Street in those ridiculous spiked helmets of theirs. Besides, he was sure it would be a great adventure.

So far it hadn't turned out that way. Training had been three boring months of drill and being shouted at by lots more red-faced sergeants. After that he'd been sent off by packed train and crowded ship across the Channel to France. Then he'd been left kicking his heels for a month at a huge base camp where the sergeants had been even worse.

He had finally been despatched to the Front in Flanders three weeks ago, but still hadn't fired his rifle, not once. He was beginning to think he never would.

'Watch out, lads,' Ernie murmured. 'Here comes the Captain.'

Alfie turned to look further down the trench. Captain Wilkins was heading towards them with Lieutenant Reynolds and Sergeant Jones just behind him. They were all dressed in the same way as Alfie and his mates, in steel helmets and scarves and thick jerkins over their service tunics, although only Sergeant Jones carried a rifle, a Lee Enfield .303 like the rest of the men – the officers had Webley revolvers in leather holsters on their belts. The Captain nodded or spoke to all the men he passed, most of whom were brewing up too. Eventually he reached the dugout and stopped.

'Morning, chaps,' he said with a smile. 'Cold enough for you today?'

Alfie liked Captain Wilkins, even though he was a toff and didn't much fit his idea of an officer, being plump, of medium height, and softly spoken. The Captain cared for the men under his command. Each day after morning stand-to he toured the line, and he always had a cheery greeting for everyone. Alfie wasn't so keen on Lieutenant Reynolds, a slight young man who was a toff too, but never said much. The lads had decided the Lieutenant had grown a moustache to make himself look older, but the wispy fluff on his upper lip had just the opposite effect. Sergeant Jones was the same as all sergeants, a bulldog of a man with a loud bark.

'Morning, sir,' said George. 'There's definitely a nip in the air.'

'At least it isn't raining,' said the Captain. 'And Jerry still seems to be keeping his head down in this sector, which is something else we should be grateful for.'

'I don't know about that, sir,' said Alfie. 'I'd like to see some action.'

'Quiet there, boy!' barked Sergeant Jones. 'Don't cheek the Captain!'

'Easy, Sergeant,' said Captain Wilkins. 'My superiors at HQ would be pleased to hear him being so war-like. You'll get your chance, Barnes, but this company has done plenty of fighting, and I'm sure your comrades have told you it was no picnic.'

'Amen to that, Captain,' muttered Ernie. George and Cyril nodded.

'Anyway, you should all be feeling rather warmer soon enough.' The Captain's smile returned. 'I've ordered a double rum ration to be dispensed.'

'Very good of you, sir,' said George. 'That should put a few hairs on our chests.'

Everyone laughed politely.

The rum ration was doled out each morning, and most of the men knocked back the small tot of foul-smelling, thick black liquid with lots of lip-smacking and gusto. Alfie couldn't stand the stuff, and wouldn't touch it.

'Well, cheerio, we must be on our way.' The Captain headed along the trench, hopping on the fire-step to avoid the puddle. 'Make sure the duckboards here are replaced today, Jones. This mud could be the death of someone.'

Alfie heard a crack like a firework going off. The Captain crumpled, his knees folding, and he fell headlong from the fire-step into the mud with a wet thud. His helmet came off, and Alfie saw a hole the size of a sixpence in his temple.

Dark blood oozed from it, and Alfie knew he had just watched a man die.

Chapter Two

The Taste of Bile

For a moment Alfie could neither move nor speak, his eyes fixed on that bloody hole in the Captain's temple. There was a swirl of movement and noise in the trench around him, men running and shouting 'Sniper!' and 'The Captain's been hit!', and a rattle of rifle fire as somebody shot back at the German trenches. But everything seemed incredibly distant, a strange dream that was nothing to do with him.

'Alfie, Alfie...' someone was saying. 'Alfie, are you all right?'

Alfie felt a hand roughly shaking his shoulder. He let out his breath with a gasp, not realising till then that he had been holding it in, and managed to tear his eyes away from the Captain. Suddenly everything was louder, brighter, more intense, the world snapping into place again. It was Ernie who had been speaking. Alfie glanced round at his friend's worried face and nodded, still unable to speak.

'Cease fire!' yelled Sergeant Jones. 'You won't hit the swine anyway.'

The shooting stopped, silence and stillness descending on the trench, and Alfie took in the scene before him. George and Cyril and several other men were up on the fire-step, Sergeant Jones to one side, everybody staring at Captain Wilkins in the trench bottom. One side of the Captain's face was covered in blood and the mud under his head was stained scarlet. Lieutenant Reynolds was kneeling next to him.

'We'd better get the Captain moved, Sergeant Jones,' the Lieutenant said at last, standing up. 'Take him to the First Aid Post. We'll bury him later.'

'Right you are, sir,' the Sergeant said quietly. 'You men there, look lively!'

Four soldiers from further along the trench came to lift the Captain and carry him away, one to each limb, the Lieutenant following them with his eyes. The Captain looked like a giant doll, limp and floppy and lifeless.

'Have the parapet checked, Sergeant,' said the Lieutenant. 'There must be a gap.'

'Spotted it already, sir,' said George from the fire-step. He nodded at a place where two sandbags had split and slipped. 'The sniper can't have seen much, though.'

'Which means he's a damned good shot,' said the Lieutenant. 'Send a runner to Battalion HQ too, Sergeant. We should tell Colonel Craig what's happened.'

'I'll go, sir,' said Alfie, finding his voice. He felt the need to do something, anything, and he wanted to volunteer before the Sergeant chose someone else.

The Lieutenant nodded, then walked slowly off down the trench, his head bowed.

'Barnes, why are you still 'ere?' the Sergeant yelled, making Alfie jump. He looked round at Ernie again, who squeezed his shoulder, more gently than before.

'You cut along, Alfie,' he said, smiling. 'We'll have breakfast ready for you when you get back. Bacon and eggs, sausages, a fried slice or two?'

'He'll be lucky,' George called out. 'It'll be bully beef and biscuit as usual!'

'See you later, Alfie,' said Cyril. 'And remember, keep your head down.'

Alfie hurried away in the opposite direction to the one taken by the Lieutenant, dodging round the other men, the buzz of what had happened to the Captain preceding him. After fifty yards of straight trench he came to a small bay set back from the front line. Just beyond that was the entrance to the main communication trench that would take him the hundred yards to the support line, and then the same distance to the reserve line, eventually emerging half a mile from Battalion HQ.

The trenches had been given the names of London streets by the men, to remind them of home, perhaps – it was a London regiment, after all. So the support line was Oxford Street, the reserve line was Piccadilly, and the communication trench was Charing Cross Road.

Alfie had only gone a few yards down the latter when he realised he would have to stop. His stomach churned and he threw up, last night's dinner of bully beef, biscuits and tea splattering onto the duckboards around his boots. He leant against the trench wall, his forehead on his arm, feeling hot and cold at the same time, the taste of bile in his mouth. His stomach was empty, but his mind was full of a single image – the small bloody hole in the Captain's head.

Captain Wilkins wasn't the first dead man Alfie had seen in the last three weeks. There was no getting away from them on the Western Front. They were everywhere: in no-man's land, buried in the walls of trenches with arms or legs sticking out, rotting under the duckboards. Alfie had been horrified at first, and shocked when he'd heard men joking about the bodies. He wasn't sure he'd ever be able to do the same. But the awful truth was that he had almost stopped noticing them.

Seeing a man killed right in front of you, though, that was different. One minute Captain Wilkins had been there, walking and talking and full of life, and the next minute – no, the next second – he had been turned into the lifeless thing those men had carried away. And everyone had been so matter of fact about it! But then as the Captain had said, the Company had done plenty of fighting. Alfie's mates and all the others must have seen lots of men killed before.

A distant rumble of heavy guns made the duckboards tremble under his feet, bringing Alfie back to the moment. This won't do, he told himself, wiping his mouth on his sleeve. He'd wanted to see some action, and by golly, he'd seen it. What use would he be to his country if he fell apart every time something bad happened? What would his family think if they could see him like this?

'Get a grip, Alfie,' he muttered to himself. He had a job to do, a message to deliver, and he was going to do it.

The communication trench came to an end in the cellar of a ruined house on the edge of a shell-blasted village. Beyond that were open fields and one of those long, straight French roads with lines of trees on either side. Battalion HQ was a ten-minute walk along it, in a mansion the Army had taken over, a large building of red bricks with tall windows, each flanked by green wooden shutters, and a roof of shiny black slates. A flight of steps led up to an imposing pair of doors guarded by two sentries.

'Urgent message for the Colonel,' said Alfie, and they nodded him through.

He had marched past Battalion HQ several times on the way to the front line, and on the way back when the company was heading for the rest area, but he'd never been inside. It was impressive, like something from a story-book. Beyond the entrance was a spacious hall half-filled by a wide staircase. There were doors that led to other rooms, he supposed, and officers everywhere, immaculate in proper, clean uniforms with shirts and ties and shiny boots, most of them carrying files or documents.

Alfie stood in the middle of the polished wood floor. He was suddenly very conscious of his own scruffy, mud-caked outfit and sick-stained boots, and uncertain where to go or what to do. One of the officers noticed him and came over.

'Looking for someone, Private?' he said. 'You seem lost.'

'Yes, sir, thank you, sir!' said Alfie, whipping off his helmet and saluting smartly. You didn't have to salute the officers in the front line, but he knew he should here at HQ. This officer – a tall man with a hard face and red tabs on his lapels – looked like the kind who would insist. 'Important message for the Colonel, sir.'

'I see,' murmured the officer, who was a major, the next rank up from a captain, and one rank down from a colonel. 'You'd better come with me, then.'

Colonel Craig was in the largest room off the hall. He was standing next to a long table covered in maps, pointing at one in particular and talking to a couple of other officers. They also had red tabs on the lapels of their tunics, as did the Colonel. Alfie stopped in front of him and saluted even more crisply this time. He had never seen the Colonel up close before, only from a distance, at a parade when he'd arrived from base camp. The Colonel was tall too, and had a narrow face and grey hair.

'Very sorry to bring bad news, sir.' said Alfie, who had thought hard about what to say. 'But Captain Wilkins is dead, shot by a sniper after stand-to.'

'What damned bad luck.' The Colonel frowned. 'He was a good man, been with the Regiment a long time. Popular with the rank and file, too.'

'I'm not sure that's always a good thing,' said the major who had brought Alfie to the Colonel. 'Wilkins wasn't the most... aggressive of soldiers, was he?'

'True, Sanderson,' murmured the Colonel. 'Perhaps we should replace him with someone who has rather more fire in his belly. What do you think, Private?'

'Me, sir?' said Alfie, surprised. Suddenly every officer in the room was staring at him. 'Er... if it means I'll get to do some fighting, then I'm all for it.'

'That's the spirit,' said the Colonel, smiling. 'I know just the man for the job.'

Chapter Three

Distant Rumbling

As Ernie had promised, breakfast was waiting for Alfie when he got back to the trench, although by then it was almost mid-morning. George and Cyril and a couple of other men were putting down new duckboards at the spot where the Captain had been killed. Ernie was in the dugout, stirring something in a tin on the primus.

'Blimey, that smells good,' said Alfie, sitting next to him. 'What is it?'

'Why dear boy, it's a stew of the finest beef and vegetables,' said Ernie in a pretend posh accent. 'Supplied to His Majesty's Armed Forces on active service by the esteemed firm of Maconochie and Co, as you can see on the side of this 'ere tin.'

'Yeah, and not for free, neither,' muttered Cyril, taking his seat beside them. 'I'd say Mr Maconochie is making a tidy old sum out of selling his stew to the Army.'

'Good luck to him,' said George. 'I just hope there's enough to go round.'

'Me too.' Alfie couldn't take his eyes off the food. 'I'm starving.'

'Didn't they offer you anything to eat at Battalion HQ?' Ernie frowned as he ladled the stew into bowls. He added a slice of white bread to each one.

Alfie shook his head, but didn't speak as his mouth was already full. The hot, fragrant stew was delicious, and of course his stomach was empty. Ernie always made sure Alfie got something to eat, usually giving him a larger portion of whatever they had because he was 'a growing boy'.

Alfie was certainly hungry most of the time. Occasionally their rations didn't make it from the rear to the front line, and an awful lot of scrounging and thieving went on. Luckily, Ernie was a dab hand at both.

'That's no surprise,' said Cyril with a snort. 'Those red-tabs are too busy stuffing their own faces to offer one of us anything. I heard they have three slap-up

26

meals every day, whatever they want, with wine for dinner. It's all right for some.'

'Yeah, well, they need to keep their strength up, don't they?' said George. 'It must be hard doing all that planning. Being here is a cushy billet compared to that.'

Cyril and George carried on in the same vein while they ate, Ernie chipping in from time to time. Alfie had often heard his mates say the same kind of things; it was clear they didn't have much time for the 'red-tabs' at HQ. But the officers he'd met this morning hadn't seemed so bad, not for toffs, anyway. Besides, somebody had to do the planning, and naturally it was the same out here as it was back in Blighty – the ones with the posh accents were in charge.

'So tell us, Alfie,' said Ernie at last. 'Who are we getting as our new captain?'

'I don't know his name,' said Alfie. 'But I do know he won't be like Captain Wilkins. The Colonel said it would be someone with more fire in his belly.'

The other three went still, their faces suddenly serious.

'Oh no,' murmured George. 'That's all we need.'

'What's wrong?' Alfie looked from one to the other and back again. 'It'll be good to have a captain who'll liven things up a bit. I mean, how are we ever going to win this war if all we do is sit around in holes in the ground? We should be taking the fight to Fritz. Everybody at home thinks that's what we're doing already.'

'Yeah, well, they haven't got a clue,' said Cyril. 'They're not here. We are.'

Alfie frowned. Every time they got on to the subject of fighting the enemy he hit a brick wall. It must be to do with whatever had happened to the Company before he'd arrived. His mates never seemed to want to talk about it, and Alfie hadn't asked. Now he decided he would have to... but he wasn't going to get his chance just yet. Sergeant Jones was heading down the trench towards them, barking orders at everyone.

'Right, you layabouts,' he said when he reached the dugout. 'If you reckon you'll be sitting around on your backsides as usual today you've got another think comin'.'

'Now there's a surprise,' said George. 'No rest for the wicked, eh, Sarge?'

The Sergeant grinned. 'Couldn't have put it better myself. I want this trench looking spick and span before the new captain arrives. Hurry up, jump to it!'

The lads grumbled and groaned, but Alfie knew they didn't really mind. The trench was where they lived for a week at a time, and it needed constant maintenance and repair to keep the men inside it safe. Even though Alfie complained about being stuck in a filthy trench, he knew it was the only way to stay alive. Modern weapons were far too deadly for armies to fight each other in the open as they had done in the old days. Machine guns could wipe out hundreds of men almost instantly.

But the trench also filled up with rubbish: empty tins and bottles and fag packets, ammunition boxes, bits of lost or discarded equipment. The battalion was divided into four companies, each spending alternate weeks in the front line or in reserve, and some companies were more untidy than others. The wind often blew stuff in from no-man's land too, and any rain turned soil into mud, undermining the sandbags and planks that held up the walls, swallowing the duckboards in the trench bottom.

There were rats as well, big, bold beasts scampering and scavenging everywhere. On his first night in the dugout a rat had run across Alfie's face as he'd been falling asleep, and he had nearly died of fright. He'd wanted to shoot it with his rifle, but that would have got him into trouble. As far as the Army was concerned, bullets should only be used to kill Germans.

Most of the men took no notice of the creatures, and as with the dead, Alfie had grown accustomed to rats being constantly underfoot. He would never, ever get used to the smell of the trench, though – a foul odour generated by months-old corpses rotting in the mud, the unwashed bodies of living men and the stench of their waste. They had no way of getting clean and no toilets, just a couple of stinking latrine pits for the whole company at the end of short 'sap' trenches leading back from the front line. Alfie loathed the latrines, and had nightmares about falling into one. But he had to use them like everyone else.

Sergeant Jones kept the men busy throughout that day, and for Alfie the time flew by. One job couldn't be done during daylight, which was why after the evening stand-to Alfie and Ernie found themselves repairing the parapet at the spot where Captain Wilkins had been killed. They worked well together, replacing any of the sandbags that had split open, making sure they left no gaps for snipers.

'There, that ought to do it,' said Ernie. 'Any sign of Jonesy?'

'No, haven't seen him for ages,' said Alfie. 'We can relax.'

Ernie sighed with fatigue. They were standing on the fire-step, but now he took off his helmet, pulled a cigarette from behind one ear, and knelt down in the shadows to light it with a match – everyone said the quickest way to get a sniper's attention at night was to be careless about such things. Ernie rose again and leaned back against the trench wall. He offered Alfie a drag on his fag, and Alfie shook his head.

The moon was bigger, but there was more cloud, so the darkness was deeper than it had been the night before. Suddenly there was a distant rumbling and bright flashes lit the sky, turning the underside of the clouds yellow and orange.

'That's coming from the south,' said Ernie, peering over the parapet. 'Sounds like Fritz is giving the Jocks a pasting. I wouldn't want to be in their shoes tonight.'

'Is it really that bad, then?' Alfie asked. The rumbling was joined by the crackle of rifle fire and the chatter of machine guns. 'Being in action, I mean.'

Ernie didn't reply for a moment, his eyes still on the gun flashes to the south. Alfie felt the fire-step beneath his feet shaking with the dull thud of every explosion.

'It was for us,' Ernie said. 'Oh, not to begin with. There was a certain amount of shelling when we took over the trench from the last mob that were here, the Royal Welch, but that was just old Fritz saying hello Tommy, welcome to the Salient, don't take this personally, and our guns gave them as good as we got. Then some bright spark at HQ decided the Battalion should do its bit, and we were ordered to attack. Four companies, a thousand men going over the top with fixed bayonets.'

To Alfie it sounded absolutely amazing, and just the kind of thing they should be doing. 'So what happened next? You can't leave the story there.'

'It wasn't a story, Alfie. It was real. We were cut to pieces by Fritz's machine guns, and then he shelled us into the bargain. We lost a lot of good men that day, and we ended up right back where we'd started. It was all for nothing.'

Alfie was shocked and wanted to argue with him. How could he possibly say that? The newspapers in Blighty had said the Germans were evil and had to be beaten, whatever the cost, and that to die in such a war would be a noble sacrifice.

But Alfie had heard the bitterness in Ernie's voice, and stayed silent.

Chapter Four

Power and Menace

The replacement for Captain Wilkins arrived after stand-to the next morning. Alfie could tell immediately that Captain Johnson was quite different to their previous commander. For a start he was tall and well built, but he had a very military air about him too, a look of steeliness as he strode down the trench, checking everything with his sharp, dark eyes.

Lieutenant Reynolds and Jonesy scurried along behind him, trying to answer his snapped questions, making note of his clipped comments.

'I've arranged for two trench mortars to be sent up from the rear, Reynolds,' Alfie heard him say in his posh voice as he strode past the dugout, raking Alfie and his mates with a brief glance of assessment. 'I want one in this section and one in section B. I'll be obliged if you could make sure they're in place by evening stand-to.'

'M-m-mortars, sir?' Reynolds stammered. 'But we've never used them.'

'Is that so?' said Johnson. 'Well, it's time we gave Jerry a surprise.'

He continued along the trench, Lieutenant Reynolds and Jonesy following. Alfie watched him go, and was reminded of a panther he'd seen on a visit to London Zoo. For a moment he couldn't understand why, and then it came to him. The panther had been full of power and menace, as was Captain Johnson, and both were confined, the animal in a cage, the man in a hole in the ground. Alfie grinned. He had a feeling the new captain wouldn't stay confined for long.

'Things are looking up!' Alfie turned to his mates in the dugout. 'He's a cool customer, and no mistake. Did you hear that? A couple of trench mortars!'

'I heard it, all right,' muttered Ernie, his face grim. 'I wish I hadn't.'

'Me neither,' said Cyril. 'If I recall, Fritz don't much like surprises.'

'Huh, that's putting it mildly.' George wasn't smiling for once.

Alfie had no idea what they were talking about. Why should they worry about Fritz? The Germans were the enemy. A sudden wave of irritation at his mates came over him. They looked ready for another session of grumbling about all the usual stuff, and he just couldn't face it, especially when exciting things were probably about to happen elsewhere. So he quietly slipped away before they could tell him to get the kettle on, and headed off to follow Captain Johnson.

The new captain's impact was visible everywhere along the line. There was plenty of muttering in his wake, but also plenty of activity as a result of his orders. The Company's four Lewis machine-guns were moved to new positions he'd chosen, and two new rearward-running saps were dug, each with a wide circular area at their furthest point from the line. Alfie soon realised these were for the mortars.

He watched a three-man Royal Artillery crew setting one up. It seemed pretty basic – an iron pipe three feet long and six inches across, with a metal plate for it to stand on and a couple of rods to support it in a diagonal position, the whole thing painted the usual drab Army green. The bombs came in wooden boxes, sinister black globes of iron twice the size of a cricket ball, with sticks attached to them like handles.

'Look like toffee apples, don't they?' said one of the Artillery men with a smile. 'They're not very sweet when they go off, though. Kill a man at twenty paces.'

Two dozen boxes were stacked behind the mortar, each one holding a dozen bombs. Alfie tried to work out the total, but he'd never been much good at sums and gave up. He only knew it added up to a lot of death.

That evening after stand-to, Alfie sat in the dugout with his mates, eating the meal Ernie had prepared. It was bully beef and biscuits again, although Ernie had managed to rustle up a couple of tins of peaches for afters. George tried a few jokes, but Cyril and Ernie weren't interested, and before long they all fell silent. Then Jonesy appeared – he always checked on the men in the evenings – and Ernie beckoned him over.

'So what do you know about the new captain then, Sarge?'

'Why are you askin' me?' said Jonesy. 'I'm not the bloomin' oracle, am I?'

'Come off it, Jonesy,' said George. 'You'll have made it your business to find out. I bet you know what he likes for his breakfast and his mother's maiden name.'

'I think you boys are mistakin' me for someone who indulges in tittle-tattle.' Jonesy scowled at them. 'Now if everythin' is tickety-boo here, I'll be off.'

'Maybe the Sergeant needs a little something to wet his whistle,' said Cyril.

Jonesy had started to walk away, but he turned to them again, raising an eyebrow. Cyril retrieved a bottle of French cognac from the rear of the dugout and handed it to him. Alfie had tried the cognac once. It had burned his throat like liquid fire, and he hated it more than Army rum. Jonesy, however, clearly had a liking for it.

'Don't mind if I do.' He took a huge swig and handed back the bottle, then glanced over his shoulder and leant further into the dugout.

'Can't tell you much,' he said, his bark lowered to a whisper. 'All I know is he got himself a bit of a reputation when he was with the Fifth Battalion, at least if the nickname they give him is anythin' to go by. They called him Mad Jack. You boys take care, now.'

Jonesy nodded a goodnight at them, then headed away down the trench. Ernie, Cyril and George exchanged dark looks. Alfie tried to keep his face blank, but it was hard to conceal his excitement. How he would love to earn a nickname like that!

The mortars were to start firing the next morning, half an hour after stand-to. The Company had been warned, and Alfie could feel an air of tension along the line as the moment approached. He bagsied one of the trench's parapet periscopes – an upright wooden box two feet high containing an arrangement of mirrors – so he could watch the attack. The first shot fell in no-man's land with a dull crump that sent a fountain of mud twenty feet into the air. The second landed well beyond the German line. Then the mortar crews found the range, and bomb after bomb dropped into Jerry's trenches. Alfie was sure he could hear screams.

After ten minutes or so the mortars fell silent. Alfie wanted to cheer like you do at a football match when the referee blows his whistle and you know your team has won by a long way. But the trench was strangely quiet. He looked round. It was empty – his mates and everyone else had vanished.

All at once Ernie's head appeared from behind the sacking over the dugout.

'For God's sake, Alfie!' he yelled. 'Don't just stand there – take cover!'

Alfie wondered why Ernie seemed so worked up. Then he heard the boom-boom-boom of heavy guns somewhere in the distance, and understood – the German artillery was opening up.

He leapt off the fire-step and dived into the dugout just as the first shells whistled down in no-man's land and behind the trench. Ernie pulled him deep into the dugout, where George and Cyril were already huddled.

'There, you see?' yelled Cyril. 'I told you Fritz don't like surprises.'

Alfie wasn't listening. He felt as if he were inside a huge drum that was being struck by a giant fist every few seconds. Each impact released a cloud of dirt from above, the soil getting into his eyes and mouth, each shockwave pulsed through the dugout walls and up through the ground. It all seemed to go on for ages, far longer than the mortar attack on the German trenches, but it stopped at last.

After a few moments, Ernie said it was safe to leave the dugout. Alfie emerged into the grey daylight with his mates, his ears ringing as if he'd been repeatedly bashed round the head. He expected to see that the whole trench had been blown to kingdom come. It was still there, although it looked as if some giant angry creature had bitten huge chunks out of the rear wall and kicked in the parapet. The trench bottom was full of smashed wood and torn sandbags, and dark swirls of smoke with a strange, bitter-sweet smell hung in the air. Alfie coughed as it hit the back of his throat.

'The smell of cordite, Alfie,' said Ernie. 'There's nothing quite like it.'

Alfie wanted to ask what cordite was, but he didn't get the chance. 'Out of the way!' someone yelled behind him, and he was roughly shoved aside.

Two men were racing along the trench carrying a stretcher with a man on it, a soldier with his eyes shut tight, his face as white as paper. He only seemed to fill half the stretcher, and for a moment Alfie thought he must be incredibly short. Then he saw that both the man's legs ended in a ragged, scarlet mess just above where his knees should have been, and that blood was pumping out of the stumps.

'Jesus wept,' muttered Cyril. 'Poor devil. Hope he makes it.'

Chapter Five

The Butcher's Bill

Seconds after Alfie had emptied his guts on his boots the trench mortars opened up again, and Ernie dragged him back into their dugout. The German artillery soon replied, and this time the bombardment was even heavier than before. Alfie huddled between his mates and curled into a tight ball, making himself as small as possible, trying not to scream or cry and desperately wishing it would all just stop.

Then the British big guns joined the exchange, and Alfie began to wonder if the noise of shelling and counter-shelling would simply get louder and louder until it crushed his skull.

It ceased at last, and after a while he and his mates

crawled out of the dugout once more. The first thing Alfie saw was Captain Johnson striding through a cloud of smoke, swirls of it clinging to him like the folds of a cloak.

'Stand to, men!' he shouted, pulling his revolver from the holster on his belt. 'This might be the moment Jerry chooses to attack, so we need to be ready for him.'

The Captain strode further on up the trench, yelling the same thing at the other men he passed. Alfie jumped onto the fire-step and waited, gripping his rifle, his heart knocking against his ribs, too scared to even think about looking over the parapet. Nothing happened, however, except for a couple of bursts of machine-gun fire further along the line, and the order to stand down was given half an hour later.

'You all right, Alfie?' said Ernie, his face full of concern.

'I'm fine.' Alfie didn't want to admit he'd been utterly terrified. His heart had slowed, but his hands were shaking and he was finding it hard to hear.

'It could have been worse,' said Cyril. 'A hell of a lot worse.'

'Oh yeah,' said George. 'It could have gone on for days.'

Alfie didn't want to think about that, and luckily he didn't have to. Orders came for the trench to be put to rights as quickly as possible, Lieutenant Reynolds and Jonesy organising the men into working parties. Alfie spent the rest of the day helping to shore up the trench with new planks, digging out the heaps of soil that covered the duckboards, shovelling it into sandbags. It was back-breaking, exhausting labour.

They took time for a brew-up in the middle of the afternoon. The trench was tidier, almost normal again, although the bitter-sweet smell lingered, overlaying the usual odours, Ernie explaining that cordite was the propellant in artillery shells. The sky was pale grey, almost white, the temperature dropping steadily, and now that he wasn't working any more Alfie could feel the cold seeping into his bones.

It was good to get the primus going, to see its blue flame lighting up the shadowy dugout, to feel its warmth on his hands. Ernie put a tot of whiskey from his small silver flask into each mug of tea, even Alfie's.

'Go on, get it down you,' said Ernie, smiling. 'You look as if you need it.'

Alfie was too tired to argue, and took a sip of the scalding liquid, expecting it to be spoilt by the alcohol. But his mouth filled with a strange sweet smokiness, and when it hit his stomach he felt a wave of warmth spread through his whole body.

They sat quietly for a while, drinking their tea. Alfie brooded on what had happened – and more particularly, on how he had reacted to the events of the last few days. Twice now he had been sick at the sight of blood, of what bullets and bombs did to men's bodies. Worse, his terror during the German bombardment had really unsettled him.

He glanced at his mates, and suddenly he felt angry with them.

'Why didn't you lot tell me what being shelled was like?' he said.

Cyril shrugged. 'There's no way to describe it, Alfie. You wouldn't have believed us if we'd tried. You have to live through it to know what it's like.'

'What's up?' said George. 'Worried because you nearly filled your pants?'

Alfie shrugged and looked down, unable to meet their gaze. 'No. Maybe.'

'Forget it,' said Ernie. 'We all feel like that, all of the time. You'd be crazy to feel anything else.

There are no heroes here, Alfie. Just the lucky – or the dead.'

Alfie knew they were trying to make him feel better, and he was grateful to them for that. He wasn't sure he entirely agreed with Ernie, though. Captain Johnson seemed like someone who could be a hero. It had been amazing to see the Captain striding out of the smoke this morning like some kind of warrior from ancient days, a Saxon or a Viking. There had been no fear in the Captain's face, none at all.

'Well, our new leader is definitely crazy,' said Cyril. 'No wonder the lads in the Fifth called him Mad Jack. He looked as if he was having the time of his life.'

'Huh, let's hope he's had enough fun to keep him happy for a while,' said George with a snort of disgust. 'Jonesy told me the butcher's bill for this morning's little entertainment was seven dead and ten wounded, a couple of them badly.'

'I heard two lads in Section B were blown to pieces,' said Cyril. 'There were just enough bits to fill a sandbag, and the working party couldn't tell who was who.'

They fell silent for a moment, Alfie struggling with the image Cyril's words had left in his mind.

It was a terrible way to die, without any chance of fighting back, like rats in a trap. He hated the idea of that happening to him. If he was going to die for his country – and he was beginning to realise he might have to – he wanted it to be when he was out in the open, attacking the enemy with his rifle in his hands.

'Cheer up, you miserable beggars!' said Ernie. 'You can all stop worrying.'

'Is that right?' said Cyril. 'So how did you work that one out, then?'

'We won't be be here much longer,' said Ernie. 'We'll be out of the line the day after tomorrow. Mad Jack can't cause a lot more mischief before then, can he?'

Cyril and George shrugged and sipped their tea, but Alfie could tell Ernie had eased their minds. Alfie was relieved too, although he felt a wave of guilt the instant he realised that. He told himself he should be keen for the Captain to attack the enemy whether Fritz retaliated or not. Yet his stomach churned at the thought of any more shelling. He wasn't sure he could take that kind of pounding again.

Captain Johnson, however, had another form of mischief up his sleeve.

Later, after the evening stand-to, the Captain came striding down the trench with Reynolds and Jonesy in his wake, the three of them stopping outside the dugout.

'Wakey, wakey in there!' barked Jonesy. 'The Captain would like a word.'

Alfie and his mates emerged, still holding their mugs of tea. Johnson stared at them each in turn, his cool, penetrating gaze like a knife, or at least that was how it felt to Alfie. The boy stood straight, squaring his shoulders, trying to show the Captain that he was a proper soldier. But the Captain was more interested in Alfie's mates.

'I understand some of you lads have seen a bit of action,' he said.

'Oh, I don't know about that, sir,' said Ernie. 'Nothing much, anyway.'

'You're being too modest, Private,' said the Captain. 'I was told you three have been in a few big shows, and done well in them, too. Isn't that so, Sergeant Jones?'

Ernie, Cyril and George turned to stare at Jonesy, their eyes hard and cold. Jonesy couldn't meet their gaze.

'Er...yes sir,' he said.

There was a brief pause, the Captain waiting for Ernie to say something else, Alfie realised. But Ernie stayed silent.

'I'll get to the point,' said the Captain, suddenly brisk. 'I'm putting on a stunt tonight, a raid on Jerry. We should keep up the pressure, and of course we need some intelligence as well. I'm looking for volunteers, men who know how to fight.'

Now you're talking, thought Alfie with a thrill of excitement. He had read in the newspapers back in Blighty about 'raids'. The idea of a small party of men staging a surprise night attack on the German trenches had seemed to him impossibly brave and dashing. None of his mates had spoken yet, but he didn't care. This really was the kind of thing he'd signed up for – the opportunity was far too good to miss.

'You can count me in, sir,' he said, saluting smartly. 'I'd like to volunteer.'

'Hang on, Alfie, you don't know what you're letting yourself in for,' Ernie said quickly. 'You'll have to forgive him, Captain, he hasn't been out here long.'

'I'm not sure you should take him, sir,' said Reynolds. 'He's rather young.'

'The Army reckons I'm old enough to fight,' Alfie declared, glaring at them both. How dare they try and stop him! 'I wouldn't be here otherwise, would I?'

'Capital!' said the Captain. 'He might be young, but he's clearly keen as mustard, and he puts the rest of you to shame. Unless you're all volunteering together?'

There was a brief uncomfortable silence. At last Ernie turned to look at Alfie. 'I can't speak for the others, sir. But if Alfie's going, I will as well.'

Cyril and George shrugged and nodded too, and the Captain beamed.

'Good, that's settled,' he said. 'This is going to be a night to remember!'

Alfie grinned. He certainly hoped so.

Chapter Six

Choose Your Weapons

It was soon obvious to Alfie that his mates didn't feel the same way. Once the Captain had gone, Cyril and George exchanged grim looks and did lots of sighing and head-shaking. Ernie was worse, though: he simply sat on the fire-step and stared into space.

For a moment Alfie felt exasperated and almost walked off again. But he didn't. Something about their expressions sent a shiver of fear running through him.

'What's wrong?' he said, looking at each of them. 'What have I done now?'

'You've just gone and signed your own death warrant,' muttered Cyril.

'And ours too, probably,' said George. 'You explain it to him, Ernie.'

Ernie raised his head, his eyes locking onto Alfie's. The guns were rumbling in the south again, lighting the evening sky with distant orange flashes. Further down the trench men were bustling around, and Alfie could hear Jonesy barking orders.

'A raid might sound exciting if you've not been on one, Alfie,' said Ernie. 'But believe you me, the only thing more dangerous out here is going over the top in a full attack. I've never known a raid happen without a few lads getting killed.'

'Well, maybe it'll just be a few Germans getting killed tonight and none of us.' Alfie pushed down his fear, turning it into anger against them. 'That's what we're here for, aren't we? And why did you volunteer if it's going to be so bad?'

Ernie almost smiled. 'Somebody's got to save you from yourself, Alfie.'

'You know, I'm fed up with you lot treating me like a kid,' said Alfie. 'I'm a soldier like the rest of you, although I seem to be the only one who wants to fight.'

'Watch your tongue, Alfie,' said Cyril, frowning. 'That's firing squad talk.'

Alfie blushed, realising he might have gone too far. He'd heard the stories about men who refused to fight being executed by firing squad. For a long time he'd thought it was all nonsense, mostly because he'd been unable to believe British soldiers would behave like that in a war. But everybody said it was true.

'Sorry, lads,' he mumbled. 'I didn't mean to accuse you of anything.'

'Forget it,' said Ernie. 'Go and ask Jonesy where the assembly point is, and whether the Captain is going to give us a briefing. It would be good to know when he plans for his little stunt to kick off, too. We don't want to be late now, do we?'

Alfie ran off, pleased to be given something to do, although that particular task was soon completed. Jonesy told him the assembly point would be a bay further down the trench, that the Captain hadn't said anything about a briefing, and that the raid itself would start at midnight. So there were still several hours to go, and for Alfie they crawled past, an eternity of waiting filled with anticipation.

'Come on lads,' he said at last to his mates. 'What's going to happen? You can't leave me in the dark again. You have to tell me so I know what to expect.'

They were in the dugout, finishing another tin of

Maconochie stew that Ernie had produced as if by magic. He and Cyril and George had eaten with their usual relish, but for once Alfie had no appetite. The only light came from a small oil lamp hanging from a hook screwed into one of the planks that formed the roof of the dugout. The lamp swayed every so often, registering the impact of distant explosions.

'A raid's a very simple thing, Alfie,' said Cyril, shrugging. 'We just crawl across no-man's-land in the dark, making sure we don't get stuck in our wire or theirs, jump into Jerry's trench and kill as many of the poor devils as we can find. It's easy.'

'Dead easy,' said George, and the other two snorted. 'Don't forget the intelligence part of it, Cyril,' he continued. 'We're supposed to have a rummage in Fritz's dugouts, see if we can find any important information he might have left there.'

'You never know, we might even come across the German High Command's plan for the war on the back of a fag packet,' said Cyril. 'Or Kaiser Bill's address. Then we can go and visit him after it's all over. I've always wanted to sleep in a palace.'

George and Cyril were laughing now, but their mood was brittle and nervous, and suddenly Alfie knew they were just as scared as him.

'All right, you lot,' said Ernie at last. 'Time to get ready.'

He took a bowl from the box where he kept his cooking stuff and poured some black powder into it from a tin. The powder was burnt cork, and Ernie mixed it with wet mud from the wall of the dugout to make a thick paste. He smeared it all over his face and Alfie's, and Cyril and George did the same. Alfie thought the four of them looked like shadows, only the whites of their eyes reflecting the lamp-light.

Then Ernie turned down the lamp and led them to the assembly point. Two dozen soldiers were already waiting there, whispering, their faces blackened too. Above them a half moon hung in a clouded sky, its eerie light lying on the men's helmets and shoulders like silver snow, their legs and feet in darkness. Several of the men nodded to the new arrivals, making room for them among their number.

'Out of the way, lads!' said a voice from the other side of the bay. Alfie recognised it as Jonesy's, as the Sergeant pushed through the group of soldiers. Two men with a long wooden box were right behind him. For an instant Alfie thought it was a coffin, and was horrified. But there was a heavy clanking sound when the men lowered their burden onto the duckboards and he realised he'd got it wrong.

Jonesy threw back the lid of the box and its contents glittered sharply in the moonlight.

'Right, choose your weapons!' said the Sergeant. There were knives and blades of every kind, some short, others as long as swords, a few with handles that would also serve as knuckledusters. There were clubs as well, a couple like maces from the days of knights in armour, others with nails sticking out of them.

Alfie gave Ernie a questioning look. 'It's no good going in guns blazing, Alfie,' he said. 'The killing has to start quietly, or we'd be sending an invitation to every Jerry in the sector. We only start shooting and bombing when it's time to leave.'

Jonesy and his helpers brought out two more boxes, the first containing Webley revolvers and ammunition, the second full of Mills bombs. Alfie had done a day's training with Mills bombs, so he'd seen the black, apple-sized hand grenades with their segmented shells before and he knew what they could do. But there had been fifty men on the course, and he'd never got round to actually throwing one.

Alfie watched as men picked out revolvers and loaded them and stuffed their pockets with Mills bombs. He knew neither were for him, but he couldn't see himself using a blade or one of those clubs either, and was relieved when Jonesy detailed him and a couple of the others to be the raiding party's riflemen. Their job would be to give covering fire if necessary, especially on the way back from Jerry's trench.

'Fix your bayonet though, son,' said Jonesy, his voice softer than Alfie had ever heard it, almost friendly. 'You might need to do a bit of close work as well.'

'Er... right-o, Sarge,' said Alfie. He pulled the foot and a half of shining, sharpened steel from the scabbard on his belt and clicked it onto the end of his rifle.

Suddenly a hush fell over the trench, and Alfie looked round. Captain Johnson had appeared, the men parting to allow him through. Beneath his helmet his face was blackened, and he had two pistols thrust into a thick belt round his waist, along with a short curved blade like a cutlass. He had two more belts crossed over his chest, each carrying extra ammunition pouches and Mills bombs. Alfie thought he looked amazing, like a pirate, and felt a thrill, half fear, half excitement.

'Everyone ready, Jones?' said the Captain. Alfie could see now that Lieutenant Reynolds was behind the Captain, and clearly coming on the raid too – he had a brace of pistols and a small hatchet stuck in his belt. But he wasn't giving off the same air of cool confidence as the Captain. He had blackened his face, but even with all that burnt cork and mud to conceal his expression, Alfie could tell he was nervous.

'Yes sir!' said Jonesy. 'Just waiting for the wire-cutting party to return.'

At that moment, three dark figures appeared at the parapet. Alfie's heart leapt into his mouth as they climbed over and jumped down into the trench. But they weren't Jerries, they were British, each man carrying a large pair of wire cutters.

'We've cleared a path, sir,' one of them said, speaking quietly to the Captain.

'Good work, chaps.' He turned to the rest of them. 'The briefing for this evening is simple. We're going to give Jerry a bloody nose and make him wish he'd never started this war. I expect you all to do your duty and fight like true Englishmen – or like devils, I don't much care which. Best of luck to you.'

He nodded, and three ladders were raised to the parapet. Alfie and his mates lined up by the nearest. 'Stay close to me, Alfie,' Ernie whispered, then started climbing.

Alfie swallowed hard and followed him into the darkness.

Chapter Seven

Stained with Blood

Alfie climbed the ladder up to the parapet then started slithering forward on his front, his rifle slung over his back. The ground was uneven and bumpy, mostly mud with occasional patches of sliminess that Alfie didn't want to think about. He knew there were plenty of bodies in no-man's land, some quite close to the trench, and he hated the idea that he might actually find himself crawling over an old rotting corpse.

More clouds covered the moon now, the darkness seeming to press down on him like a physical weight. Alfie could barely see the soles of Ernie's boots ahead of him, or the other men. They were moving quietly, but not quietly enough for Alfie. He heard every breath, every rustle, every clink of metal. How could Fritz not hear it all too? Every gun in the German trenches must be aimed at them, ready to fire...

There were plenty of obstacles as well. First, the barbed wire protecting their own trench. The 'path' cut through it turned out to be quite narrow: Alfie's sleeve was caught by the rusty barbs and he had to tug fiercely several times to release it. Then they had to crawl into and out of a series of shell craters, the bottoms filled with foul-smelling sludge or stagnant water. Finally they reached the wire in front of the German trench and crept through the gap made by the wire-cutting party.

Ernie stopped suddenly and Alfie bumped into him, scraping his nose on one of Ernie's boots. Somebody nearby was speaking quite loudly, and Alfie was about to hiss at whoever it was to shut up before he realised the language wasn't English. He froze. Two German sentries were talking to each other in the trench less than ten yards away. The clouds parted briefly to reveal the rest of the raiding party motionless as well, then Alfie saw Captain Johnson gesture to the two men closest to him. They nodded, slid forwards silently, and climbed over the German parapet.

Seconds later one of the men appeared at the parapet and beckoned to the raiding party to follow. Alfie jumped into the trench with the rest and saw the dead bodies of two Germans, one very young, sitting propped against the rear wall, their faces ghostly white, the fronts of their field-grey uniforms stained black by the blood still flowing from their gaping throats. For a moment Alfie couldn't take his eyes off them, mostly because they seemed so... ordinary. They were the enemy, of course – the monsters he knew as Jerry, Fritz, the evil Hun – but now he was close he could see they were men too, like his mates or the porters back home. Like him, in fact.

Things were happening around Alfie. Captain Johnson gave orders for the raiding party to split into several smaller groups: a couple to secure each end of this trench, one to accompany him down the nearest communication trench, another led by Lieutenant Reynolds. Alfie hoped he would be picked by the Captain, but found himself instead in the Lieutenant's group along with Ernie, Cyril and George.

'Right, this way,' whispered the Lieutenant, heading off down the trench.

Alfie followed, pulling his rifle over his head so he could hold it in front of him. It felt very long with the bayonet fixed and much heavier than usual. A hand grabbed his arm and his heart leapt into his mouth, but it was only Cyril.

'Try to stay calm, Alfie,' Cyril murmured. 'You'll be fine with us, I promise.'

Alfie nodded, then nearly tripped over another German body, this one sprawled across the trench. Just beyond the corpse was the entrance to a dugout, and as they reached it the two raiders who had dealt with the sentries emerged from within. They were both carrying nailed clubs dripping with blood, and hurried off down the trench without even glancing at Lieutenant Reynolds or Alfie or his mates.

The Lieutenant led them into the dugout, although Alfie immediately thought that was the wrong name for it. A dozen steps led down into something more like a room in a posh house, or at least a very fancy cellar. It had wooden floorboards, four beds, a couple of large chests against the walls for storage, and a table and four chairs in the middle. A big oil lamp hung from a hook in the ceiling, casting its light on three bodies face down on the floor, each in the middle of a widening pool of blood.

'Old Fritz certainly knows how to look after himself, doesn't he?' said Cyril.

'Too right,' muttered George. 'My house in Blighty isn't this comfortable.'

'Well, we're not here to comment on the decor,' said Reynolds. 'It's intelligence we're after. Find whatever you can, lads – maps, letters, notebooks, anything.'

He opened one of the chests and rummaged through it, Ernie tackling another. Cyril and George started going through the pockets of the dead men, pulling out and examining whatever they found.

Alfie stood watching, unwilling to touch any of the bodies, but then something caught his eye: a photograph in the hand of the nearest corpse. He bent down and lifted it free, carefully avoiding the dead fingers.

One corner was stained crimson with blood, but most of the picture was still clear. It showed a pretty young woman with blonde hair and a lovely smile. Something was written on the back of the picture, but Alfie couldn't read the spiky handwriting.

'Any idea what this says, sir?' he asked the Lieutenant, showing him.

'I'm afraid my German isn't very good,' said the Lieutenant, taking the photograph and holding it under the lamp so he could see the words clearly.

'*Mit liebe...* I think that means with love... *deine Frieda*. Your Frieda? That must be her name.' Their eyes met, and they both looked down at the body on the floor of the dugout.

Alfie thought the dead man must have often looked at the picture, and wondered when pretty Frieda would find out that he wouldn't be coming home.

The Lieutenant returned the photograph to the dead man, gently placing it on the floor beside him.

There was the sound of rifle fire nearby, and the soft crump of a Mills bomb exploding. The Lieutenant strode over to the steps and peered upwards.

'Time we made tracks.' He stuffed some papers he was holding into a pocket and pulled his Webley from its holster. 'Follow me, lads. Eyes peeled!'

Alfie expected to encounter the same darkness as before when they emerged from the dugout, but the trench was filled with a strange, flickering light. A German flare was dropping from the sky above them, and as he watched two more followed.

'That's torn it,' muttered Ernie. 'They'll be all over us now.'

Just then three Germans appeared out of the shadows further down the trench. One of them fired his rifle, and the bang was deafening in the confined space. The bullet whizzed over Alfie's head like a furious wasp and smacked into the sandbags of the trench wall behind him. Ernie, Cyril, George and the Lieutenant raised their revolvers and blasted away at the Germans, who immediately turned and fled.

The Lieutenant yelled, but Alfie's ears were ringing and he couldn't make out what he was saying. Ernie grabbed Alfie, and then they were heading back in the direction they had come, Cyril and George leading, Lieutenant Reynolds at the rear, continually glancing over his shoulder. Alfie's heart thumped in his chest and he couldn't catch his breath, but his hearing recovered quickly enough. There was more firing, and more yelling too, the noise seeming to come from everywhere.

Moments later they arrived at the point where they'd started. Jonesy was there with half a dozen men, several of them wounded. The face of one was a mess of blood.

'What's going on, Sergeant?' said the Lieutenant. 'Who started the shooting?'

'Ah, begging your pardon, sir, that would be the Captain,' said Jonesy. 'There were no Jerries in the communication trench so he led his group off to find some. He saw a couple and opened fire on them, which seems to have woken the rest up. I'm afraid we've taken a lot of casualties, sir. At least half the raiding party are dead.'

'I don't believe it,' said the Lieutenant. 'Where is he now, the fool?'

'Speak of the devil,' muttered George, looking round. 'Here he comes.'

Alfie turned round too and saw Captain Johnson hurrying along the trench towards them. He had lost his helmet and his eyes were wild in his blackened face.

'Right, follow me, you men!' he said. 'There are plenty more Huns to kill.'

'I'm sorry, sir, but I think we should get back to our lines,' said the Lieutenant. 'Jerry knows we're here, so the longer we stay, the more dangerous it will be.'

'What are you talking about, Reynolds?' said the Captain, breathing heavily. 'I wouldn't have let you come if I'd known you were the type to get windy.'

'I'm not being windy, sir.' The Lieutenant's voice was full of anger. 'I just don't think we ought to risk losing any more men.'

'Don't be ridiculous!' said the Captain, laughing. 'That's what they're for!'

Someone roared above Alfie and his head snapped up. The huge silhouette of a German soldier appeared on the top of the trench wall, outlined by a flickering Very light, throwing something down at them. Pistols barked then an enormous bang blew Alfie off his feet and he blacked out briefly. When he came to, the trench was full of noise again, but all he could see was Cyril's face next to his. Cyril's eyes were closed, and Alfie wondered how his friend could sleep so peacefully with such a racket going on around them.

Then a thin line of blood trickled from the corner of Cyril's mouth.

Chapter Eight

Sheep for the Slaughter

Rough hands grabbed Alfie's arms and yanked him to his feet. He saw Ernie's face looming over him, his mouth moving, but Alfie couldn't make out what his mate was saying. Beyond Ernie there was movement and shouting, rifle fire and the bangs of explosions, Mills bombs and German grenades, and smoke, lots of choking, acrid smoke, and a machine gun rattling away like something demented.

'Alfie, pull yourself together!' Ernie yelled in his face, shaking him.

'I'm... I'm all right,' said Alfie. 'But what about Cyril? Is he dead?'

'No, he isn't. We've got to get him out of here.'

Alfie could see now what was happening. The Germans were attacking along the trench from both directions, and from above it too. Lieutenant Reynolds and Jonesy were firing back with their revolvers, protecting the other survivors as they climbed a Jerry ladder someone must have found. There was no sign of Captain Johnson, but Cyril was lying at the base of the ladder, with George kneeling beside him.

'We'll have to carry him,' said George. 'Here, help me get him up.'

Ernie heaved Cyril onto George's shoulder in a fireman's lift, Cyril's head and arms hanging limply down George's back. Then George started climbing the ladder.

'You next, Alfie,' said Ernie. 'Don't crawl this time, either. Run.'

Alfie stepped forward to follow George, and suddenly realised he couldn't grip the rungs because his hands were full – he had managed to hold on to his rifle in all the chaos, although he hadn't fired a single shot with it yet. He looked at Ernie.

'Not till you're out of the trench too,' Alfie said. 'I'll cover you.'

'Just get a move on!' Ernie snapped at him.

Alfie slung his rifle over one shoulder and scrambled up the ladder, ducking as he heard the buzzing of German bullets, three smacking into the sandbags of the trench wall just a few inches from his face. At the top he flung himself into no-man's land, then pulled his rifle off his shoulder, kneeled and aimed down into the trench. Ernie was climbing the ladder now, leaving only the Lieutenant and Jonesy below.

Alfie saw movement to their left, and he fired five rounds rapid, as he'd been trained, the empty cartridge cases pinging out of his rifle. He had no idea if he'd hit anything, but he felt a strange sense of satisfaction in doing the job he'd been given. The Lieutenant and Jonesy took their chance. They each lobbed a Mills bomb, one to the left, the other to the right, and scrambled up the ladder too.

'Come on, Alfie!' yelled Ernie, and they ran as the bombs went off.

More flares whooshed up, from both sides, filling the sky with a sickly green and yellow light. Alfie could see clearly where he was going, but that only revealed the many places where he might stumble or fall or get caught in the wire. The rattle of rifle fire and the steady, deadly chatter of the machine gun grew in intensity, the rounds humming as they flew, dozens thumping into the mud around his feet.

At last Alfie glimpsed his own trench twenty yards ahead and tried to speed up, but his chest was bursting and his legs simply refused to move any faster. Ernie was beside him, dragging him along by the arm, the Lieutenant and Jonesy in front.

'Don't shoot!' the Lieutenant shouted. 'Raiding party coming in!'

Alfie felt a stab of the purest terror. It hadn't occurred to him that the men in his own line might think he and Ernie and the Lieutenant and Jonesy were the enemy and fire on them. But the Lieutenant's warning seemed to work and a few seconds later the four of them jumped down into the trench unharmed. The fire-step was manned. It looked like the entire Company had been brought out on stand-to.

George was kneeling in the bottom of the trench, holding Cyril in his arms. Alfie knelt beside the two of them and saw that George was sobbing, the tears leaving streaks in his blackened face. Cyril suddenly coughed, thick blood this time flowing out of his mouth, over his chin and onto his chest. He tried to grab Alfie's forearm but his fingers were too weak, too clumsy, so Alfie took his hand and squeezed it.

'What do we do?' he asked Ernie, not looking away from his dying friend.

'We help him,' Ernie hissed, then spoke softly to Cyril. 'You're going to be all right, mate, don't you worry. We'll get you to the First Aid Post pronto.'

Ernie pulled Cyril's jerkin and tunic and shirt open, blood flicking off the soaked fabric. The skin below was pale white, but more blood was oozing from two large puncture wounds caused by shrapnel. The German grenade had done its deadly work all too well. Ernie paused, his face grim. Cyril was panting, his ribs heaving, and he shook his head, his eyes searching for Alfie's, his expression desperate. He tried to grab the wall and haul himself up, but Alfie held on, pulling him close.

Alfie was crying now too. He rocked back and forth, cradling Cyril's head. But at last Cyril shuddered once and went still, and Alfie knew his friend was dead.

The next few hours were a blur for Alfie. He felt totally numb, unable to connect with anyone or anything. Fritz let them have it with more shelling, in retaliation for the raid on their trenches, Alfie thought, although none of it seemed to matter any more, and he barely registered the British counter-shelling in response. Then it was time for morning stand-to, but Ernie told him to stay in the dugout.

Alfie watched Ernie and George join the others on the fire-step in the dark. He was sitting on an ammunition box, looking down at his hands under the pale lamplight. They were covered in dried blood, Cyril's blood. He scraped away at it with his fingernails, but he couldn't seem to get it off. Two thoughts kept running through his mind over and over and over again. *It's my fault Cyril is dead. If I hadn't volunteered for the raid he wouldn't have gone either. It's my fault Cyril is dead. If I hadn't...*

Later that day Alfie found himself standing in a field under the cold grey Flanders sky, looking down at something else. Cyril's body had been wrapped in a sheet of tarpaulin and laid in an open grave in the Battalion's makeshift cemetery, a large field just behind the reserve line.

Several hundred more filled-in graves stretched beyond Cyril's, each marked by a temporary cross made of scrap wood. George had knocked one up for Cyril, and Alfie had pounded it into the ground at the head of the grave with a mallet, taking care that it stood absolutely straight.

Alfie, Ernie and George were on one side of the grave with Lieutenant Reynolds and Jonesy – the Captain hadn't allowed anyone else to go to Cyril's funeral. On the other was the Battalion's vicar, or 'Padre' as everyone called him. He was wearing an officer's uniform, but had a white dog collar like an ordinary vicar, a combination which seemed very odd to Alfie.

The Padre hurried through the funeral service – all that ashes to ashes, dust to dust stuff, with some noble sacrifice added in – glancing up every so often as if he was worried it might start raining. The Lieutenant muttered something under his breath, and Alfie looked round.

'For thy sake we are killed all day long,' the Lieutenant said more clearly, so Alfie could hear. 'We are accounted as sheep for the slaughter. Romans 8, verse 36.'

Alfie stared at him, but the Lieutenant wouldn't, or couldn't, meet his gaze. Then the funeral was over, the Padre putting on his helmet and scurrying away. A working party had been waiting, and the four men stepped up to shovel dirt into the grave, each spadeful of soil thumping down onto the tarpaulin. Onto Cyril.

'Come on, Alfie,' Ernie said gently as the others moved off. 'It's time to go.'

Beyond the field was the road that would take them to the rest area. The Company was waiting, ready to march, a column of two hundred men in lines four abreast. Captain Johnson was pacing up and down impatiently beside them. He had made it back unharmed from the German trench just before the Jerry shelling had begun. Fourteen members of the raiding party had been killed, all of them but Cyril left behind.

'Sergeant Jones!' the Captain called out. Jonesy ran over to him. 'Move the men out quickly, will you? I'd like us to be properly settled in billets before supper.'

'Yes sir, right you are, sir,' said Jonesy, saluting. 'You heard the Captain, lads!'

Alfie, Ernie and George picked up the packs and rifles they'd left by a tree and joined the column at the rear as the men marched off. It should have been soothing to feel the familiar rhythm of the march, to hear the sound of all those boots thumping in unison on the road, but Alfie was acutely aware of the gap

77

beside him, where Cyril should have been grumbling as usual. He couldn't get the Lieutenant's words out of his head, either. Was it true? Were they really just sheep for the slaughter?

Then he remembered the Lieutenant saying during the raid that they shouldn't risk losing any more men, and the Captain's reply: 'That's what they're for.' A solid lump of anger began to form round the grief and guilt in Alfie's heart.

Maybe Captain Johnson wasn't such a hero after all.

Chapter Nine

The Bells of Hell

Once the column had passed Battalion HQ the road was theirs alone, with only the occasional French farmer in a field watching them pass. The rain held off for the first hour, the grey clouds breaking up to let a weak sun through from time to time, and some of the lads said it definitely felt a bit warmer, a hint of spring in the air. Then a fine drizzle started, and before long they were all wet through.

After the second hour Captain Johnson gave the order to halt and fall out. The men moved onto the grass verge beside the road, slipping off their packs and sitting down to ease their feet. Alfie sat with Ernie and Cyril against a stone wall edging a field. At a nearby crossroads stood a small painted carving of Christ on the cross, his face in agony, his ribs showing through white skin, red blood running from his side.

Alfie stared at it for a moment, then looked away. He'd seen such carvings before, on every road they'd marched along, and outside the village churches. Ernie had said it was a Catholic thing, and Alfie had never taken much notice, although he'd thought they seemed a bit morbid. But now the little figure reminded him of Cyril, and suddenly his mind was full of those awful images again, of blood and pain.

Then he heard a noise, the distant sound of lorries, and soon a convoy was roaring past on the road. The lorries were piled with boxes containing supplies of all kinds – rations, rifle and machine gun ammunition, Mills bombs, mortar bombs, artillery shells large and small. Vehicle followed vehicle, hundreds of them, a never-ending metal river of destruction and death.

'Looks like someone is organising a party,' said George. 'A big one, too.'

'Yeah, well, let's just hope we don't get invited this time,' muttered Ernie.

The convoy did come to an end though, the last lorry leaving a strange silence behind it. Then Alfie heard another noise, the sound of marching boots and singing. A group of officers on horseback came into view, and behind them a column of men in clean new uniforms, their shiny helmets glistening in the rain. The officers were smiling, the men cheerfully belting out a song, one Alfie had sung with pleasure himself when he had marched up from base camp a few short weeks ago.

It's a long way to Tipperary,
It's a long way to go.
It's a long way to Tipperary
To the sweetest girl I know!
Goodbye, Piccadilly,
Farewell, Leicester Square!
It's a long long way to Tipperary,
But my heart's right there.

The column was longer than the convoy of lorries, Alfie and his mates and the rest of the men watching silently as company after company marched past. Some of the soldiers on the road glanced at those on the grass. Alfie realised he and the others must be a sight in their filthy uniforms. His was still stained with Cyril's blood.

Eventually Captain Johnson came striding along the verge, Lieutenant Reynolds and Jonesy behind him. 'Come on, men!' yelled the Captain. 'Are you just going to sit there like dummies and let these new boys show you up? Let's have a song!'

No one moved or said anything, and Alfie could see that the Captain was cross with them. Then George jumped to his feet and saluted. 'Yes sir, coming right up, sir!'

He sang in a loud, rich voice, 'The bells of hell go ting-a-ling-a-ling...' The rest of the lads in the Company joined in one by one. Soon they were all singing together, a wild choir that grew rowdier and more unruly with every line. Alfie didn't know the words, but he quickly picked them up. He was carried along by his mates, purging all their anger and misery with one voice, hurling it at Johnson, at the new recruits, at anyone stupid enough to think the trenches were somewhere you could want to be.

The bells of Hell go ting-a-ling-a-ling
For you but not for me:
And the little devils sing-a-ling-a-ling,
For you but not for me.
Oh! Death, where is thy sting-a-ling-a-ling?

Oh! Grave, thy victory?
The Bells of Hell go ting-a-ling-a-ling
For you but not for ME!

The song of the new recruits faltered and died, and the entire column seemed to turn as one to stare at the soldiers on the side of the road. George began to conduct the Company like some manic choirmaster, and before long the Captain's men were cheering and whistling and stamping their feet as they sang. Several stood up to dance with linked arms. Alfie laughed at the men's cheek, rebelling like naughty schoolboys faced with an all-too-serious teacher. The Captain glared at them and Alfie sang louder, showing him how ridiculous it all was, hooting at him for the order to be lively.

Johnson eventually stomped off, Jonesy and the Lieutenant in tow, struggling to keep straight faces.

'I don't think that's what he had in mind,' said Ernie, grinning and slapping Alfie's back.

Alfie grinned too. For the first time in days he was having fun, and it was all at the Captain's expense.

They reached the Battalion's designated rest area in the middle of the afternoon and were dismissed to their billets. At the centre of the rest area was a small village that had been fought over and heavily shelled in the early weeks of the war. Most of the inhabitants had fled, but a few remained and were happy to rent rooms to British officers. The men had to make do with barns in the surrounding countryside.

Alfie, Ernie and George went off to their billet, a large wooden barn that was part of an abandoned farm ten minutes' walk from the village. The farmhouse was half burnt down and the people and animals long gone, but the old barn was big and spacious and full of straw that made good bedding. The three of them soon settled in, Ernie getting the primus going so they could brew up and have something to eat.

'You all right, Alfie?' said Ernie. 'Not still blaming yourself, are you?'

They were sitting cross-legged round the primus in the early evening gloom, a couple of candles in dixie tins their only light. Alfie stopped spooning up stew from his bowl and looked into his friend's eyes. 'How did you know I was?'

Ernie shrugged. 'We all blame ourselves when one of our mates cops it. For something we said or did or didn't do, sometimes just for being alive when they're not. But you didn't kill Cyril, Alfie. It's the war you should blame.'

'And Mad Jack,' said George, almost spitting out the name, his voice full of anger. 'It's officers like him who do for most of the men in the line, them and those red-tab swines. None of them care if their cock-ups mean us privates end up dead.'

Ernie and George talked on into the evening, grumbling about red-tabs and the people back at home who didn't understand what was happening here at the Front. It was all the usual stuff that Alfie had ignored before. Now he listened closely.

The next morning Alfie got to do something he hadn't done in far too long – have a wash. Ernie had found a barrel of rain water behind the barn and told Alfie to strip off and climb into it, giving him a bar of scratchy soap to scrub away the weeks of dirt from his body. The water was freezing, but it felt good to be clean.

'Seeing as how you look presentable for a change, you can go and fetch us some proper grub from the village,' said Ernie, giving Alfie a handful of French coins.

'Happy to,' said Alfie. 'If you promise not to smell as bad when I get back.'

The day was crisp and bright and as he walked down the country road, Alfie tried to put everything that had happened out of his mind. He was going to buy eggs and bread and maybe even butter, then sit around eating with his mates. They were safe behind the lines, for the time being at least. There was a small market in front of the village church and, if he closed his eyes, he could almost trick himself into believing he was back in Covent Garden, listening to people laugh and joke.

He didn't even have to spend the money he'd been given. All sorts of amazing food was being handed out from the back of an Army lorry to a crowd of cheerful soldiers.

'Ah, I thought it was you, Barnes,' someone behind him said, and Alfie almost jumped out of his skin with surprise.

It was Lieutenant Reynolds, Alfie snapped to attention and saluted. 'At ease,' said the Lieutenant. 'Walk with me.' He led Alfie into the churchyard and stopped. More graves, Alfie thought, although most of the headstones were old, the French inscriptions weather-worn and covered in moss.

'Exactly how old are you, Barnes?' the Lieutenant asked, not looking at him.

'Nineteen, sir,' said Alfie, instantly on guard, his heart racing now.

'Are you sure about that?' The Lieutenant met his eyes, voice soft. 'If you are too young to be out here, then you only have to say. You wouldn't get into trouble, and you could be at home in a few days. You have my word on that.'

'I'm nineteen, sir,' Alfie repeated stubbornly. 'I just look younger.'

The Lieutenant frowned and held his gaze for a moment. 'As you wish, Barnes,' he said at last, turning to walk away. 'Let me know if you change your mind.'

Alfie almost called him back then and there. The idea of leaving this hell and not having to go back into the front line was tempting indeed. But Ernie and George couldn't go home, could they?

He did have a question for the Lieutenant, though.

'Er... begging your pardon, sir,' he blurted out. 'But did you really mean what you said at Cyril's funeral? About us all being just sheep for the slaughter?'

The Lieutenant paused. 'I'm sorry, that just slipped out. That's the problem with being a vicar's son, I'm afraid. I have a Biblical quote for every occasion.' He glanced at the church, his face taking on a thoughtful expression. 'In fact my father didn't want me to join the army at all. He brought me up to believe that I should care for my fellow man, not kill him. That I should always be my brother's keeper.'

'I'm sorry, sir,' said Alfie, confused now. 'Did your brother join up too?'

The Lieutenant smiled. 'No, he's far too young – he's only fifteen.' He paused, and Alfie felt his cheeks redden. 'The phrase is simply a figure of speech,' the Lieutenant went on. 'A way of saying that we should all look after each other. I joined up partly because I thought I would be able to look after the men under my command.'

'Like Captain Wilkins, sir,' said Alfie. 'And not like Captain Johnson.'

A silence fell between them. The line of the Lieutenant's jaw tightened, as if he wanted to say something and was resisting the temptation. The guns were rumbling somewhere in the distance, but it was impossible to tell whose they were.

'Captain Johnson is a very brave man,' said the Lieutenant eventually.

Then he turned away once more, and walked off without looking back.

Chapter Ten

The Shadow of Death

After three days in the rest area Alfie almost began to feel normal. His nerves were still on edge and he found it hard to sleep, his dreams full of images from the last few weeks that easily turned into nightmares. But the horrors faded in the morning light, and he spent most of his waking hours roaming the countryside, enjoying the calm of a small wood where he climbed the trees, forgetting everything for a while.

Ernie clearly wasn't happy. To begin with Alfie assumed he was still suffering because of Cyril. But then they all were, and Alfie soon realised it was more than grief. Ernie was worried about something else – and that worried Alfie too.

'What's wrong, Ernie?' he said at last. They were in the barn, eating the dinner Ernie had prepared. 'You've got a face like a wet week in Margate.'

Ernie sighed. 'The word is that we'll be getting an invitation to the party after all. I asked Jonesy and he reckons it's definite.'

'He doesn't always get it right.' George's face was serious now too. 'I heard it's going to be happening further south, to help out the French.'

'Maybe,' said Ernie. 'But I wouldn't bet on it. All the signs are there – Battalion HQ isn't making us work, they're leaving us alone so we can build up our strength. And they're giving us plenty of great grub, too. We're being fattened for the slaughter.'

There was the Lieutenant's word again, thought Alfie. Ernie was right. That lorry had been in the village every day, and had been joined by two more. Alfie had never been as well fed, but now he felt sick, and put down his dinner unfinished.

'So you reckon we're going to be in an attack,' he said. 'Like the raid.'

Ernie and George glanced at each other.

'Yes, I think we're going to be in an attack, Alfie,' said Ernie. 'But it's going to be bigger than the raid. A hell of a lot bigger.'

Early the next morning the Battalion was summoned to a parade in a field outside the village, the men forming up by company behind their officers and sergeants. Alfie stood in the front rank between Ernie and George, with Jonesy, Lieutenant Reynolds and Captain Johnson in front of them. Tension seemed to hover over the assembled men like an invisible thundercloud. At last a group of officers on horseback arrived: Colonel Craig, Major Sanderson, others Alfie recognised from Battalion HQ.

'ATTEN...TION!' yelled Jonesy as the officers reined in their mounts, his command echoed by the other sergeants. The men did as they were ordered, a thousand booted right heels thumping down on the mud, a thousand chins snapping upwards.

'At ease, men,' said Colonel Craig, raising his voice so everyone could hear. 'I won't keep you long today, but I wanted to bring you some excellent news...'

'Don't tell me,' whispered George. 'Fritz has surrendered and we're going home!'

Ernie smirked and Alfie snorted with bitter laughter, loud enough for Jonesy to hear. Jonesy turned to frown at him, and Lieutenant Reynolds looked round too, his eyes holding Alfie's for a second. The Captain seemed not to have noticed.

'...I know you're all as keen as me to show Jerry what we British are made of, and you're about to get your chance,' the Colonel was saying. 'There's going to be a big push in this sector, one that will finally knock the Hun for six. And because one of our brave officers has recently proved that the Battalion has plenty of fighting spirit, I'm delighted to say the Commander-in-Chief has agreed to us taking the lead.'

The Colonel nodded at Captain Johnson, who did his best to look modest. Alfie could feel Ernie bristling with anger beside him.

'Fourteen dead to prove that,' Ernie muttered. 'Fourteen, including Cyril.'

Your officers will brief you on your tasks, and I'm sure you'll be doing some training,' the Colonel went on. 'I'm also sure that you will do your duty for King and Country and honour the great tradition of the Regiment. Carry on.'

The Colonel saluted, and the sergeants yelled 'ATTEN-TION!' again as the staff officers rode off. The men weren't dismissed and allowed to return to their billets, though. They were to be briefed immediately about the attack, the Big Push.

It was done by company, each captain explaining to his men the overall strategy in which they were to play a part. Alfie and his mates and the rest of their company squeezed into a small hall behind the village church and listened to Captain Johnson. He summarised the intelligence that had been gathered about the German units they would encounter, pointing as he did so at a large map of the German trenches that had been pinned up on the wall. He also said there was to be a massive bombardment first, three days of heavy shelling before they went over the top and attacked.

'Which means, of course, that all the Huns will have been blown to pieces,' said the Captain with a grin. 'We can simply stroll across and capture their trenches, then next stop Berlin! The cavalry will be waiting behind us to complete the breakthrough.'

'That's good, isn't it?' Alfie whispered to Ernie. 'We'll be all right, won't we?'

'You saw how deep Jerry's dugouts are,' said Ernie, whispering too. 'It doesn't matter how heavy the shelling is, they'll survive it. As soon as the bombardment stops they'll come back up into the trench with their machine guns and wait for us.'

Alfie felt his stomach turn over at the thought of walking towards a trench-full of Germans pointing machine guns at him, and found it hard to concentrate on the briefing after that. It didn't last much longer, but there was more to come the next day. There were briefings about objectives, strong-points in Jerry's system they were to seize by certain times, and what signals they should use to send messages.

The shelling began on the following day. It wasn't the usual dull rumble that Alfie had almost got used to, but rather the angry roar of a giant, a furious rolling thunder that went on and on and made the ground shake beneath your feet and your teeth ache. Alfie thought about what it had been like to be under bombardment, and he knew this would be much worse, however deep your dugout might be.

Things moved quickly after that: weapon and kit inspections, ammunition and Mills bomb distribution, the march back to the trenches the day before the attack was to take place. Nobody sang this time, the Company swinging down the road in almost total silence, each man lost in his own thoughts. They spent a cold, wet night in the reserve line, a thousand men with rifles and full packs crowded together, trying to sleep, all of them failing. The guns were still roaring, the sky full of the sound of shells whistling down to explode a few hundred yards away.

Alfie sat huddled between Ernie and George, clutching his rifle. Further down the trench a man was muttering a psalm, starting again as soon as he finished, one line sticking in Alfie's mind: 'Yea, though I walk through the valley of the shadow of death I will fear no evil...' Another man was moaning and rocking back and forth where he sat. Others were praying, or trying by candle-light to write last letters to their families. Somebody else was going round with a sack, getting men to put into it whatever money they had to be shared out by the survivors after the attack.

'This is mad, totally barmy,' Alfie muttered. 'We're all going to die, aren't we?'

Ernie turned to look at him and squeezed his shoulder. 'I'm not going to lie to you, Alfie. There's a good chance you're right. But you never know.'

'I just hope it's quick and clean,' said George. 'And that Mad Jack cops it too.'

'I'm with you there, George,' said Ernie. 'I'd like to blow his head off myself.'

Alfie huddled down even further, remembering when he'd reported to the Colonel that Captain Wilkins had been killed, and the Colonel had asked him for his thoughts about a replacement. If he had known then what he knew now, Alfie told himself, then he would have begged the Colonel to keep Captain Johnson as far away from him and his mates as possible. Not that it would have mattered. The whole war was crazy, and the Colonel might have found them a captain who was worse.

Just before dawn Jonesy came down the trench, telling the men it was almost time. The guns fell silent, the absence of their roar shocking, the only noise now the soft murmuring of the men, the clicking of bayonets being fixed. Ladders were raised to the parapet and queues formed at their feet, the men waiting as the sky slowly grew lighter in the East, the sun rising over the battlefield.

Alfie shuffled forward with Ernie and George, a memory of trying to get on a packed London bus coming to him. This was one bus that none of them should be getting on.

Just then Captain Johnson arrived with Lieutenant Reynolds. The Captain strode along the trench, Webley in one hand, a whistle in the other, both on lanyards round his neck. 'Right, my lucky lads!' he said, grinning, raising his whistle. 'Remember, advance slowly, keep well spread out, and give them hell! Everyone ready?'

Something snapped inside Alfie. If this was madness, then why were they doing it? He turned away from the ladder and moved back through the crowd.

'No, we're not,' he said, looking Captain Johnson in the eyes.

Then he threw his rifle down between them.

Chapter Eleven

Alfie's Choice

Further down the trench in both directions Alfie could hear voices and the clink of equipment and the scrape of boot-soles on wooden rungs as men started climbing onto the ladders. But a pool of stillness had formed around him and the Captain, everyone nearby staring at them in tense silence for several heartbeats. Then Jonesy came bustling through the crowd, roughly pushing the others out of his way.

'Come on, son,' he said, stopping in front of Alfie, his voice gentle in the way it had been when he'd spoken to Alfie on the night of the raid. 'That's no way to speak to an officer, is it? Now be a good lad and pick up your rifle. We've got a job to do.'

'You're wrong, it's not a job,' said Alfie, his eyes still fixed on the Captain's. 'It's slaughter, that's what it is. He's going to get us all killed, and for nothing.'

'Arrest that man and have him removed, Jones,' said the Captain. 'We can't afford to waste any more time listening to riff-raff like him spreading sedition.'

'I hardly think there's any need for that,' Lieutenant Reynolds said hurriedly, pushing his way through the crowd too. 'Especially as it will mean that...'

'He'll be court-martialled and shot?' said the Captain. 'Well, good riddance – it's no more than the little coward deserves. I've half a mind to shoot him myself.'

Then Ernie was beside Alfie, holding his arm and whispering, his voice full of urgency. 'Don't give him the satisfaction, Alfie. Pick up your rifle and come with us. At least that way you'll have a chance. We'll take care of you, I promise.' Then Ernie turned to address the Captain. 'Sorry sir, he'll be all right once we get going.'

'What are you talking about?' Alfie yelled, trying to pull himself free of Ernie's grasp. 'Cyril's dead because of him. None of us are going to be all right.

We'll just get slaughtered so he can get another pat on the back from the red-tabs. I'm doing this for you, Ernie, and for George, and for everyone else who doesn't need to die!'

'That's enough,' snapped the Captain. 'Sergeant Jones, I gave you an order.'

'Er... yes sir,' said Jonesy. He grabbed Alfie's other arm, but Alfie shook him off and advanced on the Captain, Ernie desperately trying to hold him back. Alfie stepped over his discarded rifle, his boots skidding on the muddy duckboards,

'How many died when you were playing with your mortars, sir?' Alfie yelled, spit flying from his mouth, the last word filled with hate. 'How many men died on the raid because of you, sir? How many are going to die this morning, sir?'

'You'd better get him under control, Sergeant Jones, or I will,' the Captain said coldly. He stood his ground, raising his revolver, aiming it at Alfie's chest.

Alfie didn't care. He screamed abuse at the Captain, using the foulest swear words he could think of. Out of the corner of his eye he saw a movement, something swinging towards him, and a light seemed to explode inside his skull. He fell to his knees, then onto his front, the back of his head throbbing with intense pain, and he realised that Jonesy must have hit him, probably with the butt of a rifle.

He heard shouting somewhere and there were boots too close to his face and his mouth was filled with mud. He felt hands under his armpits, two men lifting him back to his feet. His vision was blurred, huge faces looming in and out of sight around him, their mouths open and yelling, the Lieutenant and Jonesy and George and sad-eyed Ernie, the ladders behind them, and he tried to speak but couldn't.

He blacked out, his head falling forward onto his chest, and when he came to he was being dragged away, his boot tips bumping and thumping over duckboards. His first instinct was to struggle, to try and break free from the men gripping his arms, but they were too strong and he could do nothing but shake his head and groan. Suddenly a new noise cut through the fuzziness of his mind and filled it with pure anguish.

Someone was blowing a whistle, a high, clear note that was soon joined by the sound of cheering. Alfie could see in his mind what was happening, a thousand men swarming up the ladders, going over the top, advancing into no-man's land. Then he heard the chatter of machine guns, and the cheers instantly turned into screams.

The Big Push had begun.

The two men holding Alfie dragged him to the end of the communication trench where they persuaded the driver of an empty ammunition lorry to give them a lift to Battalion HQ. They threw Alfie into the lorry and sat on either side of him, both men immediately taking out fags and lighting them. Alfie lay there, the back of his head banging painfully on the floor with every jolt as the lorry crawled down the road.

He was beginning to feel a little more alert by the time they arrived at HQ and he was taken in through the familiar main doors. Inside, staff officers with sheaves of papers hurried past, all far too preoccupied to take any notice of them. At last one of the men holding Alfie attracted a major's attention, and a brief conversation ensued. Moments later Alfie was handed over to a couple of burly military policemen.

They took him to an office where they made him empty his pockets and asked him his name and serial number. They wrote both down in a big ledger. Then they led him to a small bare room with a tiny, high window and no furniture, and locked him in. Alfie sat down in the corner, back against the wall, knees drawn up to his chest, his head still throbbing but clear, and wondered how much longer he had to live.

It all seemed so pointless. He hadn't changed a thing. The attack had gone ahead, and he had simply guaranteed that he would be executed for cowardice. He had wanted to be a hero, but he had brought shame on his family instead. Alfie started to cry quietly. He should have kept his mouth shut. At least then he would have died with his mates.

Hours passed. A military policeman brought him a bully beef sandwich, a mug of tea and a bucket to pee in. Another came with a couple of blankets when the light had gone from the window. Alfie wrapped himself in the blankets and lay down, his mind full of images – Ernie and George and Cyril laughing, the dead German soldiers in the raid, the picture of Frieda, Captain Johnson's face – but he fell asleep in the end.

It was the door opening and the Lieutenant coming in that woke him.

'You're free to go, Private Barnes,' he said. 'You will face no charges.'

Alfie rose to his feet. 'I... I don't understand,' he said. 'The Captain...'

'The Captain is dead,' said the Lieutenant. 'Along with everyone else.'

The light in the room was still dim, but now Alfie saw the Lieutenant was more plastered with mud than usual. The left side of his face was covered in dried blood, and he looked exhausted. He removed his helmet, placing it on the floor and fumbling in the chest pocket of his tunic for a silver cigarette case and lighter. His hands were shaking as he took out a cigarette, but he got it lit, inhaling deeply.

'What happened, sir?' said Alfie. 'In the attack, I mean.'

'The usual total and utter shambles, of course.' The Lieutenant's voice was full of anger and bitterness. 'Jerry was waiting for us with his machine guns as soon as we climbed out of the trench, and they cut us down like wheat in a field. No one made it even as far as the Jerry wire, and not a tenth made it back. I saw things that will stay with me forever.' He paused and took a deep breath. 'I was lucky, I suppose.'

'And my friends, sir?' Alfie said. 'Did Ernie and George make it?'

'I'm sorry, Barnes.' The Lieutenant shook his head. 'They were hit early on, as was Sergeant Jones, and nearly everyone else who heard what passed between you and Captain Johnson. He's dead too, which means there are very few witnesses.'

Alfie thought about Ernie and George and Cyril and Jonesy and everything they had done for him, and he hoped their deaths had been as George had said, quick and clean. Strangely enough he found himself hoping it had been the same for Captain Johnson. But then nobody deserved to die in filth and agony, not even Mad Jack.

'The two men who brought me here heard it,' he said. 'They told a major and he told the military police, so I don't understand how you can say I'm free to go.'

'You have a trump card to play – your age. Oh yes, it was fine to sign up lots of brave under-age boys at the beginning, but they're getting killed and parents are kicking up a stink. So now the Army wants rid of you all. I've already spoken to Colonel Craig, and he says the choice to go or stay is yours. If it was up to me I'd have you out of here and your way back to Blighty in the next few minutes.'

'But the choice is mine?' asked Alfie. 'And I won't be court-martialled if I stay?'

'No, you're safe,' said the Lieutenant. 'The Colonel has other things on his mind.'

Alfie closed his eyes and thought about the journey home, the march to the rail-head, the train full of soldiers, the ferry, another packed train into London, seeing his mum and dad and his brothers and sisters. Then he thought about the new soldiers who would be coming to replace those who had died. The men who would need someone to take care of them just the way Alfie's mates had taken care of him.

It was the easiest choice he would ever have to make.

Historical Note

There were many boy soldiers like Alfie in the First World War – or The Great War, as it was called until the Second World War followed it 20 years later. Thousands of boys lied about their ages to enlist, some as young as 14. Before the war the minimum age for joining the Army was officially 18, and you had to be 19 to be on active service, but there had long been a tradition of recruiting sergeants and officers allowing themselves to be 'fooled' by boys eager to join up. In 1914 and 1915, the early years of the war, huge numbers of men rushed to enlist, and those doing the recruiting were not likely to turn away enthusiastic volunteers, even if they were clearly very young indeed.

Of course, few of those who were volunteering to fight knew what war was like, and nobody understood what 'modern' weapons – heavy artillery, machine among the officers and men themselves. Someone like Lieutenant Reynolds might even have gone so far as to make a protest in the same way as Siegfried Sassoon, a lieutenant and one of the famous poets of the war. He threw a medal he had been awarded for bravery into the River Mersey while he was on leave, and refused to fight. He did go back, although only after the Army had sent him to a hospital for soldiers with 'shell-shock'. Most soldiers fought on, although usually that was because they didn't want to let down their fellow-soldiers, their 'mates'. Sassoon said he went back partly to look after his men – although they gave him the nickname 'Mad Jack' because he was an enthusiastic raider of the German trenches.

There are many other books available if you're interested in finding out more about the First World War. Richard van Emden's *Boy Soldiers of the Great War* is excellent, and in its pages you will encounter the real boys who were like Alfie – many of whom were killed. We would also recommend the famous memoirs of the war written in the years after, *Goodbye to All That* by Robert Graves, *Memoirs of an Infantry Officer* by Siegfried Sassoon, *Undertones of War* by Edmund Blunden. Everyone should also read the work of the great war poets – Sassoon himself,

Wilfred Owen, Edward Thomas, Isaac Rosenberg, Ivor Gurney. And finally, there are several websites well worth checking out: the Imperial War Museum at *www.iwm.org.uk/centenary*, The National Archive at *www.nationalarchives.gov.uk/pathways/firstworldwar/* and the BBC at *www.bbc.co.uk/history/worldwars/wwone/*.

Tom and Tony Bradman

World War I Unclassified

From the assassination of Archduke Franz Ferdinand to the signing of the Treaty of Versailles, *World War I Unclassified* takes readers on a journey back in time to discover the amazing story behind one of the most terrible wars in history.

Photographs and original documents from the National Archives are reproduced along with artifacts and documentation that enable readers to build a true and real account of World War I and how it shaped the world.

ISBN 9781472905253   £10.99